The Signalman: Two Ghost Stories

Written by Penny Dolan

Illustrated by Stefano Tambellini

Collins

The Signalman

There were few trains at night, so I wasn't expecting
the bell on the telegraph to ring. I heard it, glanced
across the signal box, then realised the metal bell was
not shaking.

"No!" I gasped, tears of terror flooding my eyes.
What did the warning mean this time?

The telegraph messages had always been simple and clear. The bells told me whenever a train was coming down the line. I'd take my lantern outside and make sure the tracks were clear. I'd check that the round signal lamp by the tunnel was alight. Then, while that red glass eye glared out its warning, I'd watch the fiery train thunder out from the gaping mouth. I was never afraid, not then.

Then, one night, the first message came. The bell's
eerie echo made me stare at the telegraph machine.
I was terrified when I saw that the bell wasn't moving.

What was the ghostly sound telling me? I didn't know.
So I carried on, doing my duty as a signalman.
What else could I have done?

I went outside. I shone my lantern up and down the track, wondering whether an unexpected train was coming. Then I froze. A tall figure stood beside the tunnel. Silently, it raised one long arm, covering its face, as if it was trying to tell me something.

What was it warning me about? Trembling, I walked towards it, growing colder and colder and –

Suddenly, there was nothing, only an empty space. *Where had the figure gone?* I ran into the tunnel. I shone my lantern wildly about. All I saw were the slimy walls, dripping with water. Nothing more.

With dread in my heart, I staggered back to the signal box. Never had I been so glad to see daylight return.

Nevertheless, back in my lodgings, with breakfast inside me, I felt better. I told myself that I'd fallen asleep and had a bad dream. I decided to take an old arithmetic book with me the next night and do some sums to keep me awake. It worked. The next night passed peacefully.

Then came the third night! The strange bells started jangling, filling me with dread. An hour later, I heard a terrible sound: an explosion! I ran out, afraid to look. Deep inside the tunnel, a train had crashed. There was nothing but fire, smoke and screams and staggering figures. As I raced towards that awful scene, longing to help, I recalled that strange figure. *Had it tried to foretell this disaster?*

Even so, time moved on. The strange bells seemed silent and everything was as before. Slowly, my fears faded. *If only things had stayed that way!*

Yes, one night, the bells began jangling a second time. I could hardly bear it; but I did what I had to do. I went outside.

The figure was there by the tunnel, silently weeping and wailing. As I walked closer, it covered its face with long pale hands. I lifted my lantern, ready to ask . . . But, with a scream of grief, the shadow had gone!

What was the message? Would there be another crash? No. The disaster, when it came, was very different.

On the third night, as I waited beside the track, a train passed by, with lights shining brightly from the carriages. I glanced up at a window. Suddenly I saw a terrible tangle of arms, hands and torn hair within. I swear I heard a terrified woman scream.

"Stop, stop!" I yelled, waving my flag furiously and signalling with my lantern. Something terribly bad was happening on that train. Was I the only one who had heard the cry for help? However, by the time the train stopped, it was too late. The guards carried a covered shape past me on a stretcher, and a sharp shiver shot down my spine.

Worry, cold as ice, filled my heart. *Should I have told someone there'd been a warning?* What a hopeless idea! If I told the Railway Company I'd seen visions, I'd lose my job at once. *Perhaps I'd say something if it happened again? Yes!* So I kept quiet and a month went by, although I worried night and day.

I was almost glad when that dreadful
bell started jangling again. Scared though
I was of that shadowy shape,
I had to go and look. Would I be able
to work out the message this third time?

The figure was down by the tunnel, eyes glittering in the red glow of the signal lamp.

"Look up!" it shrieked, waving one arm wildly. "Look up! Look up!"

I ran forward, shouting. "For pity's sake, tell me what's going to happen!"

As if in answer, it closed those dreadful eyes – and was gone. The only voice was mine, echoing within that terrible, hollow tunnel. For a while, I stood there, sick with fear.

At last, I turned, half in a dream. I trudged slowly back along
the track, deciding what to do. As soon as I reached
my signal box, I'd find a pen and ink and write to
the Railway Company. I'd tell them about the messages
and the visions, no matter what happened afterwards.
Someone there would know what to do, they would!
All at once, my weight of worry left me.

I returned, and wrote my letter. I had only one last task to do
that night.

I crunched along the cinder path and checked the oil in the red lamp. I saw no figure at all. Weary with relief, I plodded steadily back between the rails, and —

The Engine Driver's Report

It was an accident, sir, a mysterious accident. The signalman was on the track, sir. I leant out from the engine, waving and shouting. I yelled "Look up, Look up!" as loudly as I could. He didn't look up, sir, not even when the wheels were almost on him. I didn't want to watch so I flung one arm across my face. I kept calling "Look up! Look up, you down there!" But he never did.

The Face on the Train

The gallery was empty, apart from one old man. He looked at me with a crooked smile.

"You paint so many famous people, sir," he said. "Is there any face you remember? Is there?"

Shivering, I clutched at a chair. There's only one face I see.

Years ago, when I was a young painter, a letter came, inviting me to paint a portrait. There weren't many details but, because the house was in a beautiful part of the country, I replied at once. I never imagined what the strange journey would bring.

I packed my colours, sketchbooks and a few good clothes,
then I walked to the busy railway station. No sooner
had I taken my place in the crowded compartment
than the whistle blew and the train was on its way.

For a while I sat there, my mind full of the work ahead. I had a good eye so the first sketches would be easy enough. I'd always had a talent for capturing faces and figures in a few swift lines.

I learnt about my subject in these early sittings. *What did they want their portrait to look like? What did they want it to say?*

Only when I knew things like that could the portrait painting begin. I'm glad I didn't know what lay ahead.

After an hour or so, the train arrived at a station. All the other passengers got out. Pleased to be alone in the compartment, I stretched out my legs, gazed out at the scenery and drifted off to sleep . . .

I woke, startled, feeling cold. While I slept, the train must have stopped at another station. A young woman now sat in the opposite corner, away from the sunlight. She wore good travelling clothes and hid her face behind a veil. This train must be unusually crowded, I thought, because a lady travelling alone wouldn't usually enter a compartment containing a single man.

I spoke, so that she'd feel safer. "Good afternoon",
I said, blushing. "Please excuse me for not getting up
when you entered, Miss."

She nodded her head a little, in greeting. I sensed she was
smiling at me. Then – and I don't know why – I started to tell
her about my art. I unstrapped my case and spread out my
half-painted sketches for her to look at.

"See," I said, chattering on, "here is *this* person. And here is
that person. Here is *so-and-so*, who's a famous beauty . . ."

I know I boasted a little. I wanted her to know I was a real artist. She picked up each sketch and studied my work.

She spoke softly, half-laughing. "So many faces! Do you remember them afterwards?"

"Not really," I admitted. "I move on to the next."

"Could you remember this face afterwards do you think?" she asked gently, and drew back her veil for a moment. "Could you?"

I stared, seeing only her beautiful smile, her remarkably bright eyes and her pale, pale skin. A second later, the train entered a short tunnel. Then there was my station.

As I stuffed my sketches back into my case, the woman stepped lightly down on to the platform. I tried to follow her but she'd disappeared among the smoke and the shadows. I didn't even know her name.

That night, I stayed in the Railway Hotel but sleep didn't come. *"Could you remember?"* Long after midnight, I covered page after page of my sketchbook, trying to capture that bright, smiling face once more. As I fell asleep, pencil in hand, I thought I heard the woman's gentle laugh.

Thankfully, the morning's coach ride lifted my spirits.
Even so, as I walked into the beautiful house, I sensed
something was missing.

My host was unwell, so his daughter, Maria, greeted
me in the library. She welcomed me warmly, although
there was sadness in her kind, plain face. We spoke,
over tea, about the house and gardens.

At last I said, "Miss Maria, your letter wasn't very clear. Who does your father want me to paint? Is it you?"

She laughed and shook her head. "No. Papa can see me any time he wants. What he longs for is a portrait of my sister, Lucy." She paused. "She's not at home any more."

I was surprised to hear that nobody would be sitting for the portrait. Where had Lucy gone? Had there been a family quarrel or was she living overseas? I didn't pry, and Maria didn't explain.

"Is there a picture that I can copy, then?"

"No," she answered. "That's why we need the portrait."

"Is there a photograph I can use?"

"Only this." Maria opened a leather-bound album.
Inside was a photograph showing three figures: a kindly
old man and two girls. One was Maria,
but the other girl's face was not at all clear.

My heart sank. "I don't think I can do what you want,"
I said, sadly.

Maria placed her hand on mine. "Please listen.
My father has his heart set on this portrait.
We discussed how it could be done."

"How?" I was truly puzzled.

"You're an artist, sir, aren't you?
If I described my sister carefully,
surely you could draw what
I tell you, couldn't you?
Isn't it worth trying?
This could be my
father's last wish."

She seemed so hopeful.
How could I refuse?

For five days I did try. Maria described every feature
of her sister's face. Then I drew as best I could.

"That's it! That's right," she cried happily, after I'd
sketched a nose or ear or eyebrow or lock of hair.

Nevertheless, whenever I drew the whole face together,
something seemed wrong.

"It's like her," Maria said sadly, "but it's not her.
Something's missing."

By the sixth afternoon, I couldn't stand it any longer. "I'm sorry,"
I said. "I can't do what you want, Miss Maria. I'll leave this evening."
The portrait mattered so much to them and I hated failing.

"Please, go tomorrow," she begged. "My father's a little better.
He'd like us to eat together tonight."

Dinner was pleasant, although the old man barely spoke. Afterwards,
as we took him to his study, he murmured something in Maria's ear.

"My father would like to see some of your other work," she said.

"Certainly!" I said, keen to make the evening more cheerful. "I've got some interesting landscapes, and studies of the lions and reptiles in the Zoological Gardens, too."

Moments later, as I carried in a big pile of sketchbooks, disaster! One slipped, then another and suddenly all my paintings and drawings cascaded down. The floor was covered with places, faces and all sorts of creatures.

I gathered my work together as quickly as I could, arranging
the loose pieces across the study desk and tables.
All at once, the room felt strange.

Maria, still as stone, was staring at my midnight sketches.
"Where did these come from?" she asked. "You didn't
do these here, did you?"

"No," I said, taking the sheet. The sketch was better than
I'd remembered. "She was a girl I met on the train."

"When?" Maria's voice trembled.

"On my journey here," I said.

Tears glistened in her eyes. "Then you saw my sister?"
she said. "My dead sister."

I gasped. Now I understood their sorrow.

"She died a year ago to the day," the old man whispered.

I didn't know what to say.

Maria broke the silence. "Sir, can you remember her face once more?" she asked. "Well enough to paint the portrait?
It would heal our hearts to see Lucy here again.
Can you remember her? Can you?"

"Yes," I said. After all, that was what Lucy had asked me to do.

In the days that followed, I painted wildly, desperately, remembering that strange meeting.
Eventually, her portrait was
hung in her old home.
Maria and her father
were content.

But me? Now I'm never content. Each night her veiled face haunts my dreams. I wake, and must paint and paint till dawn.

Train journeys

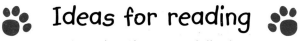

Ideas for reading

Written by Clare Dowdall, PhD
Lecturer and Primary Literacy Consultant

Reading objectives:

- identify themes and conventions

- discuss their understanding and explain the meaning of words in context

- ask questions to improve understanding

- make predictions from details stated and applied

Spoken language objectives:

- participate in discussions, presentations, performances, role play, improvisations and debates

Curriculum links: Art – drawing and painting

Resources: percussion instruments, digital recording equipment, paper and pencils, ICT for research

Build a context for reading

- Look at the front cover. Ask children to recount any ghost stories that they know. What can they see happening in the illustration?

- Read the back cover blurb aloud. Explain to children that this is a retelling of two Charles Dickens tales, and that he was a famous Victorian author who wrote *A Christmas Carol* – a well-known ghost story.

- Check that children understand what a signalman and portrait painter are, and what their jobs involve.

Understand and apply reading strategies

- Focus on the opening of *The Signalman*. Read pp2–3 aloud. Help children to build their understanding of the context and the meaning of the words *telegraph, signal box,* using discussion and questioning.